Night Letters

by PALMYRA LoMonaco

pictures by NORMAND CHARTIER

DUTTON CHILDREN'S BOOKS • NEW YORK

Text copyright © 1996 by Palmyra LoMonaco   Illustrations copyright © 1996 by Normand Chartier
All rights reserved.
Library of Congress Cataloging-in-Publication Data
LoMonaco, Palmyra.   Night letters/by Palmyra LoMonaco; illustrated by Normand Chartier.—1st ed.   p.   cm.
Summary: Lily goes into her backyard after supper and takes notes on what the insects and natural objects have to tell her.
ISBN 0-525-45387-3   [1. Nature—Fiction.   2. Night—Fiction.]   I. Chartier, Normand, ill.   II. Title.
PZ7.L8415Ni   1996   [E]—dc20   94-36988   CIP   AC
Published in the United States 1996 by Dutton Children's Books, a division of
Penguin Books USA Inc.   375 Hudson Street, New York, New York 10014
Designed by Adrian Leichter   Printed in Hong Kong   First Edition
1 3 5 7 9 10 8 6 4 2

21,75

To my mother, who taught me to read
night letters when I was a child,
and to my husband,
who reads night letters with me now
P.L.

For L. Rubia, Sally Rubia,
and special thanks to Kate Considine
N.C.

Night letter time.
When supper is over
and the dishes are done,
when the clouds blush raspberry red,
and a faraway harmonica
plays a low, sleepy song,
I know that night letter time
has come.

I put my purple notepad and pencil
in my backpack and set out
to gather the letters
my backyard friends write
telling me about their day.

There are zigzag lines in the dirt that I can read.

Dear Lily,
My children and I picnicked
on bread crumbs and sesame seeds
that you dropped from your lunch.
Thank you.
> *Very truly yours,*
> *the Ant Family*

My first night letter.
I copy the words onto my pad,
put it in my backpack,
and walk on.

A hawkmoth rests
on a crisp blade of grass.
Quietly, I bend to read
what is written on its wings.

Dear Lily,
Each evening I sip
sweet nectar from the flowers,
then I flutter my wings
and move on.
Very truly yours,
the Hawkmoth

I copy the words onto my pad,
put it in my backpack,
and walk on.

The cracks in a rock
in the tomato patch say,

> Dear Lily,
> Today I touched dew
> and a spider's web.
> Now I look for stars.
> Very truly yours,
> the Rock

I copy the words onto my pad,
put it in my backpack,
and walk on.

The fireflies switch on their flashing lights,
and if I watch without blinking,
I can read their code.
Dot-dot-dot…dot-dash…dot-dash…

Dear Lily,
Come play night sky tag.
Lights on, we're here...lights off, we're there....
Catch us if you can.
　　　Very truly yours,
　　　the Fireflies

I copy the words onto my pad,
put it in my backpack,
and walk on.
I come to the big old sycamore tree
and sit on the cool earth around her.
My hands rub her scratchy bark, and
I feel the strips left for me to read.

The tree is old, and she has much to say.
Some words are happy ones.
They tell of chirping birds
and budding leaves
and children
balancing on her branches.

Some words are lonely ones.
They tell of birds flying south
and leaves blowing away
and children staying in their houses,
and a time too cold for night letters.

When the faraway harmonica
no longer plays its low, sleepy song,
and the winds howl instead,
I will tramp through the snow,
over leaves long fallen,
knock icicles from the tree's limbs,
and wait for night letter time to return.

But right now,
as the sky fades to blackberry blue,
I read my last night letter.

> *Dear Lily,*
> *Please climb me tomorrow.*
> *Very truly yours,*
> *the Sycamore Tree*

I copy the words onto my pad,
put it in my backpack,
and walk on.

Then I turn back to the sycamore tree.
"Yes," I say,
"I promise to climb you tomorrow."
And I'll think about my day
and what to say to my backyard friends.

Very truly yours,
Lily